SUPERTATO

CARNIVAL CATASTRO-PEA!

I dedicate this book to myself
because everyone else is a NITWIT!

- Evil Pea

SIMON & SCHUSTER
First published in Great Britain in 2019
by Simon & Schuster UK Ltd
1st Floor, 222 Gray's Inn Road, London, WC1X 8HB
A CBS Company

Text and illustrations copyright © 2019 Sue Hendra and Paul Linnet

The rights of Sue Hendra and Paul Linnet to be identified
as the author and illustrator of this work
have been asserted by them in accordance with
the Copyright, Designs and Patents Act, 1988

A CIP catalogue record for this book is available
from the British Library upon request

978-1-4711-7172-7 (PB)
978-1-4711-7173-4 (eBook)

Printed in Italy

1 3 5 7 9 10 8 6 4 2

SUPERTATO
CARNIVAL CATASTRO-PEA!

by Sue Hendra
and Paul Linnet

SIMON & SCHUSTER

London New York Sydney Toronto New Delhi

It was night-time in the supermarket
and our fearless crime-fighting hero
was having to gather ALL his strength . . .

. . . to tie up some party balloons!

The veggies had been busy preparing
for the Supermarket Carnival for months.

"There you go, Carrot. This place is looking amazing!

How's the banner going, Cucumber?"

"I'm just off to get some more paint, Supertato."

"Thanks to all your hard work," said Supertato, "this carnival is going to be a wonderful celebration of colour and fun!"

But **someone** had other ideas. "That's what **you** think," sniggered the Evil Pea from his hiding place.

BAD SCIENCE

"I **hate** colour and I **hate** fun. Let's see those nitwits try and celebrate when I unleash this!"

"EVERYONE!" shouted Supertato.
"Can I have your attention, please!
It's the day we've all been waiting for.
I now declare this carnival . . ."

" . . . RUINED!" screeched the pea as he leapt onto the stage. "Behold my new invention – the Colour-Suck-A-Tron-5000.

It's going to suck the colour out of everything!

Now, who wants to see it in action?" he squealed,
as he pointed it at Carrot and Pepper.
"NO!" screamed the veggies.

"And who wants to be next? How about you 'Red' Chilli? Or should I just call you Chilli from now on?

No more green for you, Green Bean!

Goodbye Blueberry, hello Greyberry!" cackled the pea.

He was out of control. And the veggies knew it.

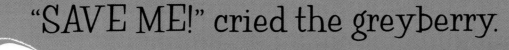

"SAVE ME!" cried the greyberry.

"SAVE US ALL!"

But who could help these veggies in distress?

There could be only one . . .

UMM . . .

"There might be a problem there, veggies. I'm feeling rather washed out myself."

"What's he done to us, Supertato?"
"I don't know, Tomato."
"I'm not Tomato, I'm Orange!"
said Orange.

The supermarket was a sad sight – the balloons
and banners, the flags and costumes,
everything was ruined.
"Why did you do it, pea?"

"Well, Supertato, I'm glad you asked," hissed the pea.
"It's not easy being mean . . .
but **someone's** got to do it!

Mwah ha ha ha ha!"

And with that,
off he sped to wreak
more havoc.

"Hmmm, looks like the end for the carnival,"
said one pineapple to the other . . .

"Hang on a minute,
look who's just walked in!"

It was Cucumber.
"I've found the paint, Supertato!"
But then she froze. "What's happened here?"

"THERE YOU ARE, CUCUMBER!" said Supertato.
"The pea stole all of our colours but you may just
have given me a great idea . . ."

"Blueberries, I'm going to need your help.

Cucumber, I'm going to need your green paint."

There wasn't a moment to lose.

So Cucumber painted the blueberries,

which wasn't easy.

Carrot gave them some masks,

Tomato gave them some acting lessons

and Supertato gave them a speech.
"Find that pea, pretend to be his evil pea
friends and let's get our carnival back!"

The Evil Pea didn't suspect a thing.

"About time!
This is really heavy,"
spat the pea as he handed
them the Suck-a-Tron.

"Well, go on then, point it at something!"

So they did.

And once the pea was in position, it was time to flick the switch from colour-sucker to colour-blaster.

It wasn't long before . . .

Tomato was
red again,

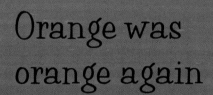

Orange was
orange again

and Supertato was that
potatoey-colour-that-doesn't-
have-a-name again.

Everything was as it should be,
and it was time . . .

... for the Carnival!

"There you are, Blueberries!
Goodness me, you have been busy.
That's the most colourful thing I've ever seen!
What a shame that Evil Pea isn't here to see it.

I wonder where he could be . . . ?"